A Purrfect Home for Kitters

Story by Jacqueline H. Faber   Illustrations by Valery Larson

A purrfect Home for Kitters is dedicated to the memory of Kelly Bane, who called all cats "Kitters," and to my cat-loving mother, Helen Grace and, of course, Tabby.

Granny calls me Kitters. We live in our *purrfect* home.

I tickle Granny's arm with two toes. *Scritch, scratch.*
It's our secret code for tuna—my favorite. I eat every bit and lick my paws.
I zoom on soft carpets. *Zip, zip, zoom!*

One morning, Granny's daughter Jackie visits. The three of us are snuggled up, watching hummingbirds hover and dart—our favorite.

But why are there tears in Granny's eyes?

"You know Jackie, I've always dreamed of a life at sea. I can sail away soon, but I can't take Kitters with me."

My ears go flat. Who will brush my coat? Who will pet my head?
Who will feed me tuna?
Who will snuggle me?

"Jackie, you love Kitters. Can she stay with you?"

"I'd love to take Kitters home. We'll both miss you, Mom, but we're happy for you too."

No! Not *purrfect!* I claw my scratching post.

Jackie stuffs me in a box. I *meooooow,* I *screeeech,* I *groooowl!*—
all the way to her house.

I leap out of the box and *swoosh*.
No carpets?
No zooming. Not *purrfect*.

I give her my two-toe tickle. Nothing! I herd her into the kitchen.

Where's my tuna?

No! Not *purrfect*.

Day after day, she brushes my coat too hard. She never scratches my itchiest spot. And I miss my tuna. Not *purrfect!*

Sometimes I hide.

One morning, she finds me. She stuffs me in the box.
"We're going to visit my friend Gary," she says. "He loves cats.
You'll like him."

At Gary's house, I leap out and land—on carpet! *Zip, zip, zoom.*

I jump onto his table.

I jump onto his couch.

I jump onto him. I swish my happy tail.

He brushes my coat softly. He finds my itchiest spot.
He feeds me tuna. Everything is *purrfect*.
        Until . . .

Jackie taps the box. "Kitters, time to go!"
No. Not *purrfect!* Time to hide.
Behind the couch? Nope.

In the closet? Nope.

On the window ledge? Yes!

Whoosh.
Yoooowl. Meoooow! Meoooow!

Gary saves me!

He holds me in his arms.

"Kitters is scared.
Can she stay with me?" he asks.

"Sure," says Jackie.
"I'll pick her up tomorrow."

Oh, happy tail!—a sleepover. Gary brushes me again.
He holds the brush while I scratch my itchiest spots. *Purrrrrr.*

We cozy up. He feeds me more tuna. *purrfect*!

The next day, I hear Jackie's voice.
I race to the closet and hide,
but she finds me.

I sprint behind the couch.
I spring to the top of the refrigerator. Nooooo!

I leap into Gary's lap.

Purrrrr!
Purrrrrr!
Purrrrrrr!

"I think Kitters wants to stay with you, Gary," Jackie says.
"I love Kitters too," he says. "She can live here as long as she wants."
I lick and lick his hand.

Jackie kisses my head. "Kitters will be happier here.
I'll miss her, but I'll visit often.
"I think Kitters understands. I love her enough to let her go."
Purrrrrr, purrrrrr, purrfect!

Now, Gary and I snuggle every day.

When Jackie visits, I rub against her legs and *purr.*

The three of us watch hummingbirds hover and dart.

And Jackie tells us happy stories about Granny.

"I love you, Kitters," Jackie says.
I bump her head with mine. I love her too. And—I get to live with Gary!

"Pretty Kitters. Pretty Kitters," they sing to me.

"Purrrrrr, purrrrrr, purrrrrr," I agree.
My new *purrfect* home.

Feline Facts

Cats usually purr when they feel happy and peaceful. Sometimes if they are hurt or scared, they purr to help calm themselves.

Cats meow loudly when they are scared and softly when they are happy. Meowing is the main way cats let people know what they want. How they meow varies by breed and individual.

When they're angry they yowl, hiss, and growl.

A cat's tail indicates its mood.

A cat's ears go back flat when it's nervous, angry, or defensive.

Cat's ears have 32 muscles to turn, even backwards, toward sounds.

A cat's tongue is rough with pokey barbs called papillae ("puh-PILL-ee"). A cat uses its tongue like a brush to remove dirt and loose hair, and to make its coat neat.

Cats can see better at night than humans, with 6-8 times more cells in their eyes that detect light.

Cats can't see under their noses, but neither can we!

Annoyed—moving quickly back and forth

Frightened—hanging down

Cats use their whiskers to determine the size and texture of objects, especially in the dark, and if they can fit in a tight space. They even feel changes in air currents to detect approaching danger.

Usually cats have five toes on each front paw and four on each back paw, but some cats have more.

A cat's heart beats 140 to 220 times per minute, much faster than a human's, which beats only 60 to 100 times per minute.

Healthy adult cats sleep from 13 to 20 hours a day. They eat, play, and explore the rest of the time.

Thinking—moving slowly back and forth

Happy—Flag is up!

CAT'S
choice
Tuna

Kitters

My name is really Tabby, but you can call me Kitters. I once belonged to Granny, but had to live with Jackie, who petted my head too hard, petted my coat too soft, and fed me broccoli. Can you believe broccoli—for a cat! But then— something great!

On a visit to Jackie's best friend, Gary, we fell in love! He pets me just right, feeds me tuna, and his lap is purrfect.

Purr, purr, purrfect!
Meow!

Jacqueline Faber

taught elementary school in Marin County for thirty-one years. She received the Golden Bell Award in 1999 for her outstanding work in "Project-Based Learning." She taught the gifted-writing program for Ross Valley School District and is a member of the Society of Children's Book Writers and Illustrators, and the Bay Area Independent Publishers Association.

A Purrfect Home for Kitters is Jacqueline Faber's second picture book about life seen through the eyes of a cat. It's based on a true story and thirty-seven years of loving, teaching, and reading picture books to elementary school children. Jacqueline has seen how exposure to good literature and inspiring illustrations can thrill children and change their lives.

Valery Larson

remembers all the wonderful cats that have found a home with her over the years. Capturing them on paper with pencil and watercolor has helped bring Kitters alive.

Valery studied classical realism and illustration at Atelier Lack in Minneapolis, Minnesota. She is a member of the Society of Children's Book Writers and Illustrators. She works in a little cottage in the redwoods, north of San Francisco.